Lord Jim

JOSEPH CONRAD

Simplified and brought within the vocabulary of
New Method Supplementary Readers Stage 5 by

FRANCES JOHNSTON

Illustrated by Ivan Lapper

LONGMAN

LONGMAN GROUP LIMITED
London

Associated companies, branches and representatives
throughout the world

This edition first published 1976

ISBN 0 582 53420 8

Filmset in Hong Kong by T.P. Graphic Arts Services
Printed in Hong Kong by Yu Luen Offset Printing Factory Ltd

Contents

1

A DREAM OF THE SEA

Young Jim sat on top of a cliff. It was a summer day and the sea below him was calm and blue, shining in the sun. In his hand he held a book, his favourite kind of book, telling stories of adventure and of the brave deeds of sailors who sailed all over the world in ships. The day was warm, and Jim soon put down his book and lay dreaming of the great deeds that he himself would do when he was a man. He gazed out to sea, watching a ship far away on the horizon, just one lonely ship.

He thought, 'That's where I would like to be! How I would love to be a sailor!' He was sixteen years old, and he knew that soon he would have to make up his mind what sort of life he was going to lead. His father was a priest and did not have much money, and he also had two other sons who were younger than Jim, so Jim knew it would help his father a great deal if he could start to work as soon as possible.

'There's no better way to live my life. A ship my home, and all the world to be seen!'

Suddenly he jumped up. He picked up his book and started to run home. He was so pleased with his idea that he felt he must get back as soon as possible. He wanted to ask his father if he could go to sea and become a sailor.

He found his father in the garden. 'Father,' he said, 'I have decided that I would like to be a sailor. I am sure it is what I would like to do most of all.'

His father said, 'Well, I am pleased by your choice. You have decided on something very suitable. You know that I am not a rich man, and there are your brothers still to educate. I will try to get you a place in a merchant service training ship for officers.'

'Merchant service?' said Jim. 'What's that?'

'It is the name given to the ships and the men who sail them that carry produce like food supplies and machinery and, yes, *passengers* too, to all the seaports in the world.'

Jim was very happy that his father agreed to help him to become a sailor.

2

THE TRAINING SHIP

Very soon after this, Jim was sent to the training ship. Here he learned all the arts of sailing a ship. He was liked by most of the other boys and the officers. He was a tall young man and very strong, and he was often sent high up the *mast* as a "look-out" because of his steadiness and strength. As "look-out", his position was high up on the mast where there is a small platform for a sailor to stand and keep watch on the sea all around. He is the first to see another ship or some danger ahead, and it is his job to call out and warn the captain. Jim often looked down from this high post. The training ship was in port and tied up safely, but instead of seeing the houses and smoking chimneys of the town near the port, he imagined the wide empty sea, perhaps a stormy sea where he would be a *hero*, and in his mind he lived the sea life of the brave men in the books of adventure that he used to read at home.

'One day, I shall do some great deed of courage, and everyone will see how brave I am!' So he dreamed—he was always a hero in his thoughts. He always thought of himself as better than anyone else, with all the courage of the heroes in the books that he read.

One stormy day, when Jim and most of the other boys were below *deck*, there was a shout from above.

'Something's happening! Everybody on deck—hurry!' All the boys ran quickly up to the deck. Jim followed them, and then, when he was on deck, he stood still—unable to move—suddenly full of fear. It was nearly dark on a winter's day. The wind was strong and the rain was pouring down. Jim looked round, trying to see what was happening. It looked terrible. Many ships had come into the port for shelter, and the strong wind was throwing them about in a most dangerous and frightening way.

The captain shouted: 'Put a boat out!'

The boys moved quickly to obey, as they had been trained to do, but Jim still could not move. He went on gazing at the dreadful sea in terror. He saw that two boats had run into each other and that one of them was sinking. There were men struggling in the water. The water was too rough for swimming and they were shouting for help.

'There, straight ahead of us.' The captain was pointing. 'Lower the boat!'

The boat moved away from the ship, with the boys in it fighting to row the boat through the rough water.

Jim ran to the side of the ship and watched the waves breaking over the little boat.

He heard the shouting. 'Row boys, row hard if you're going to save anyone!'

Then Jim felt a hand on his shoulder. 'Too late, young man.' It was the captain of the ship.

Jim looked at him and was ashamed.

The captain smiled. 'Better luck next time. This will teach you to think more quickly and to act at once!'

3

HEROES

There was great excitement as the little boat came back to the training ship with two men saved from the sea. Everyone on the ship cheered loudly, the boys were heroes as they told their story. A boy with a face like a girl's and big grey eyes was eagerly giving his account:

'I saw his head in the water and I threw out my *boathook*, it caught in his trousers, and I nearly fell into the water myself; someone held my legs and I pulled him in. The boat got half full of water, I thought we would sink!'

Jim had lost his fear by now. He felt angry with himself and with everything. He had wasted his first chance to prove to everyone how brave he really was.

'Well,' he said to himself, 'I certainly would not behave like these boys. Perhaps it's a good thing I didn't go. I think I have learned more how to act next time, by watching these stupid boys.' And so he comforted himself that he was not a coward.

4

THE ACCIDENT

After Jim had spent two years in the training ship he was ready to go to sea.

'Now,' he thought, 'life will be full of the adventures that I have been waiting for.'

He made many voyages. He always worked hard, and he learned to bear the hardness of life at sea and to win the friendship of the men he worked with. But his life seemed to be dull. He was disappointed. One lesson that he had not learned was that the only reward for a man of the sea is a great love of his work and of the oceans on which he sails. Sometimes he wished he could give it all up and go home, but something always held him and made him stay.

'I think it is the sea,' he thought. 'After all, I think I should miss the sea too much if I went and lived on land again.'

Quite soon he got a job on a very fine ship as *chief mate*. His captain said to him, 'You are young to be a chief mate. But we will see, I have great hopes of you. You are very good at your work. It is true that I have not had a chance to see you working in bad weather, but I do not doubt your courage. I'm willing to give you a chance, and I'm glad to have you on my ship.'

Then came a terrible storm. It raged for several days. There was no time for sleep and the men became tired out. Everyone had to be on deck without rest to battle against the wild sea that was trying its best to wreck the ship.

When the storm was worst, part of a mast fell on Jim. As he lay on deck he felt a terrible pain in his leg, and he knew he was badly hurt. Some of the men carried him to his bed.

'You have a very badly broken leg,' said one of the sailors, 'and you'll have to stay here. Some people have all the luck: now you can sleep!' Jim was in too much pain for any rest, but he was secretly glad that he did not have to be on deck any more in the dreadful weather.

When the storm was over the captain came to see him.

'Man! it's a wonder that the ship did not sink,' he said. He looked at Jim and examined his leg. 'Well,' he said, 'you'll have to stay in bed until we get to port. Your leg doesn't look good to me.'

5

EASY LIFE, EASY MONEY

When the ship arrived at an Asian port, Jim had to go to *hospital*. It took a long time before his leg was really strong again, and by that time his ship had sailed away without him. There were only two other men in the room where he was in the hospital. One was an officer from a warship who had also broken a leg. He had fallen down an opening from one deck to the deck below.

The other man had some mysterious disease caught in the East, which the doctor did not seem to be able to cure.

They spent long lazy days. They told each other the story of their lives, or played cards, or just lived through the day without saying a word.

The hospital stood on a hill and the gentle warm wind came through the windows. Jim's days at the hospital passed like a peaceful dream.

As soon as he could walk without the aid of a stick he went into the town to see if he could find a ship that was sailing for home.

He met another sailor who was also looking for a ship.

'But why go home?' said this man. 'Why go back to the cold stormy seas and to hard work? It is much easier out here in the East. You have short voyages, and many more sailors to do the work. Stay here in the East and have an easy life!'

'Yes,' said another sailor who had come up to them to listen. 'This is the life. The ships belong to the Chinese, and to Arabs. They will sometimes end your employment for no reason, if they do not like the look of you, but it's easy enough to find another ship.'

Jim began to think seriously about all this talk and advice. 'Easy life, easy money!' Well, why not? The idea of doing so well with so little danger to face pleased him. He decided to stop trying to go home, and took the first job offered to him, as chief mate of a ship called the Patna.

The Patna was an old ship, narrow and rather unsteady.

One of Jim's friends said, 'As old as the hills, and just look at her—rust and with hardly any paint.' The Patna was owned by a Chinese trader, but he had hired her out to an Arab for a special voyage.

The captain was a German who had lived in Australia for most of his life. He was a very fat, bad-tempered man who cared little for his crew and still less for his passengers.

He said to Jim, 'We are taking on eight hundred pilgrims, on their way to Mecca. They are coming on board now. Look at them—just like cattle!'

Jim looked at his captain. He did not like what he saw, a great fat man with a blue nose and a red beard. He also did not like the way he spoke about his passengers. They were streaming on board, urged on by faith and the hope of heaven. Silently they flowed forward, filling the ship like a living *cargo*—a cargo of human beings instead of goods. At the call of an idea they had left their homes. Their leader, an Arab, came on last. He walked slowly on to the ship, good looking and solemn in his long white Arab clothes.

When everybody was on the ship the captain wasted no time in leaving the port. He shouted his orders to untie the ropes, and the Patna made her way across the bay and *steamed* straight towards the Red Sea.

Each morning the sun rose with a silent burst of light at exactly the same distance behind the ship. It came up above her at midday and sank into the sea in front of her in the evening. The ship was travelling west on the same point of the compass all the way.

Every day there was the same flat sea; the air was hot and heavy, without a breath of wind, and the ship steamed steadily on her way, lonely on an empty sea. Each night descended like a cool blessing on the ship, on the pilgrims, and on the crew.

There were five Europeans on board. They lived separately from the rest of the crew. There were the German captain and Jim, the first and second *engineers*, and a man called George who helped the engineers with the engines below decks.

Jim was on duty on the *bridge* one night. His thoughts as usual were full of the great deeds of courage that he alone would do. He dreamed of success. In these imagined accomplishments he spent the best hours of his life. He smiled happily to himself when he thought how great a hero he would be one day.

On the deck below him, all was quiet. The pilgrims were sleeping. They slept on mats, on the bare decks, on every deck, in all the dark corners. Some of them clothed in rags, with their heads resting on their small bits of luggage, or with their faces pressed to bent arms; the men, the women with children; the old with the young; the weak with the strong—all equal before sleep, the great leveller. And two of the crew *steered* the ship. Silent, almost without movement, they stood, one each side of the wheel. So the sleepy hours passed. The Patna made a

slight whispering sound as she passed over the calm sea, leaving behind her a white line of waves on the water.

6

'WE'VE HIT SOMETHING!'

The captain came up to the bridge at midnight. His face was red and he was only half awake. He was a most unpleasant sight as he bent over the compass and scratched himself sleepily.

'Why does he have to come and spoil this lovely night?' thought Jim. 'He really is a nasty sight.'

The second engineer came up from below. He said, 'It's hot below. It's terribly hot.'

Jim smiled, but he did not look round, and the captain in his usual rude way took no notice.

'It's all right for you up here,' said the second engineer.

'Be quiet!' said the captain fiercely.

'Oh yes; be quiet, and when anything goes wrong, we get the blame!'

Jim looked at him and thought, 'He must have had a drink or two to talk to the captain like that.'

'You've been drinking. Who gave it to you?' said the captain.

'Not you, captain. You're far too unfriendly. You would rather let a man die than give him a drop. I've only had one drink, and that's the truth.'

'That engineer—your friend the chief—he gave it to you, I suppose. He must be mad to give you a drink.' The captain was angry.

Jim looked at the two of them. Neither of them meant anything to him—he was just not interested in them.

'Who's drunk?' said the engineer. 'Not I. No, no, captain, that won't do. If I thought I was drunk I would jump over the side—drown myself. I am not afraid of anything that you can do.'

The captain threatened him, but the second engineer went on talking. 'I don't know what fear is. I'm not afraid of doing all the work in this *rotten* old ship. It isn't safe— it's an old wreck, but I'm not afraid.' He took his hands off a bar that he had been holding to keep himself standing up. He threw his arms apart bravely.

Suddenly he fell forward as if he had been struck from behind. He cried out as he fell, and then shouted in pain— he had broken his arm. Jim and the captain had also fallen forward in the same minute, saving themselves before hitting the deck.

They stood astonished, gazing at the sea.

'What was that? What happened?' They looked at each other. The second engineer got up and then fell again on the deck.

'What's that?' he murmured.

'We've hit something!' the captain shouted.

There was a faint noise like distant thunder, then the ship seemed to rise a few inches all along its length as if it had passed over something in the sea. Then all was quiet again and she steamed on.

'Like a snake sliding over a stick,' thought Jim.

7

THE END OF THE 'PATNA'

The captain and Jim still stood, eyes wide with shock, unable to move. Then suddenly the captain shouted to

Jim, 'Go forward! Go and see what has happened. See if there's a hole in the ship. Go quietly. Don't say anything to anyone. We don't want the people to get frightened and start running all over the ship.'

'Yes, sir,' said Jim. He was indeed thankful that the captain was being so sensible. He took a lighted lamp that was hanging near and went forward.

When he opened the door which led to the very front of the ship, he saw that the space there was already half full of water. He knew then that whatever had struck the Patna must have made a big hole below the water level.

Jim just stood looking—he didn't know for how long. The shock of what had happened, and just what it would mean, reached his mind slowly.

'All those people,' he whispered, 'lying there asleep—knowing nothing—three times as many people as there are life-boats for—even if there was time to save them—to wake them—to get them to the boats.'

He wanted to shout, and to make all these people leap straight out of sleep into terror. But such a sudden sense of his helplessness came over him that he could not make a sound.

The second engineer came up behind him and looked. 'Heaven help us—that rotten side! It will give way in a minute, and the whole ship will go down under us like a stone.' He pushed Jim aside and ran up the ladder, shouting as he went. The captain rushed at him and knocked him down. He spoke to him angrily but very quietly. 'Go and stop the engines, man. If you make a noise like that again, I'll knock you senseless. Get up! Run! Run!' The engineer got up and slid down the ladder again, moaning as he ran, and holding his broken arm.

Meanwhile Jim ran to the bridge to find his captain. The Patna had a long bridge deck, and all the boats were up there, four on one side and three on the other. It was Jim's duty to keep them ready for instant use, and he was always most careful to see that this was done. Now he thought there was very little time before the ship must sink. He must cut the ropes holding the boats so that when the ship went down the boats would float free.

First he reported to the captain and said, 'There is water coming through a large hole up forward. We must do something quickly. There is no chance of saving the ship.' But the captain just stood thinking and doing nothing.

Jim said again, 'Captain, there are many people there, still asleep, knowing nothing. We haven't enough boats for them, the division between the forward part and the main part of the ship is going to give way, and we shall sink in a few minutes when the water rushes in.'

Jim's knees shook with fear as he stood looking down at the sleeping crowd. The engines stopped. It was so quiet, surely it would wake them all up. He thought, 'They look dead, and perhaps they soon will be dead. Nothing can save them. Eight hundred people and seven boats!' The words seemed to hammer in his head over and over again 'Eight hundred people and seven boats! Eight hundred people and seven boats!'

Again Jim asked the captain, 'Sir, there is not time to save the passengers, what must I do?'

At last the captain suddenly moved. He ran to one of the boats and started untying the ropes to let it down into the water. Jim did not feel any fear now, he ran up to the captain.

'Ah, it's you,' said the captain. 'Help me, quickly!'

'Aren't you going to do something?' Jim asked.

'Yes—I'm getting out—quick—help me.'

Jim did not move or speak. He did not understand what the captain meant. Then the two engineers appeared, and started helping the captain with the boat. Jim looked at the calm sea, black and deadly, waiting to swallow the sinking ship.

8

JIM DESERTS HIS SHIP

The two seamen who still held on to the wheel which steered the ship did not seem to be afraid. They watched the captain and the engineers struggling to get the boat free. Jim thought, 'No, they can't just take a boat and leave us all to sink with the ship!' But this is just what was happening.

One of the engineers ran up to him. 'Come and help! For heaven's sake, man, come and help!' He was pulling at Jim's coat and cursing. 'Come on! Won't you save your own life? You coward, come on and do something!'

But Jim just gazed at him. He felt trapped. It was hot and there was not a breath of air. Then he took out his knife and went towards the other boats and started cutting them free.

'You silly fool!' the captain shouted at him. 'You're wasting time. How can you possibly save everybody? Come over here and help us with this boat.'

But Jim kept away. He hated these men. He decided to keep as far away as possible. He wouldn't help them to escape—to run away in this shameful way. He couldn't bear it any longer and he shut his eyes. When he opened them again there were four men trying to get the boat free to drop it in the water; George had come up from the engine room to see what the two engineers were doing. A sudden storm blew up, and the ship started to rock as the wind got stronger.

'Let go! Let go! The ship is sinking. Let the boat go into the water!' They let go of the ropes and the boat at last fell down into the sea. The four men rushed forward to jump into it, but one of them suddenly fell on the deck and stayed there, not moving.

'Jump man, jump! Oh, jump quickly! We can't wait!' But the fallen man lay still.

And then, suddenly, Jim ran forward and threw himself into the waiting boat. Why? He did not know; he found himself there with the men he hated. He looked up at the ship—his ship—with despair in his heart. He now knew that he really was a coward. 'I wish I could die!' he cried. But it was impossible to go back. He felt as if he had fallen into a well, an everlasting dark deep hole from which he would never escape.

9

JIM IS UNWELCOME

They rowed the boat away from the ship. The storm was passing and the sea was quieter. Jim looked back, the ship was still floating. 'It's terrible to see them still there,' he thought. 'All those people still have to drown. —please God, make it happen quickly!'

Everybody in the boat was silent. It moved steadily away from the Patna. Then somebody cried out: 'She's gone!' They all stood up to look.

'There are no lights, nothing except darkness. She has

gone!'

'I turned my head just in time, I saw her go down,' said the engineer. They all talked then.

'I knew from the first that she would sink.'

'We got away not a moment too soon.'

'A lucky escape indeed!'

Only Jim said nothing. They all turned towards him.

'What stopped you jumping, George?'

'Why were you so slow, you fool?'

Jim realised that they thought it was their friend who had jumped into the boat with them, the man who had fallen on the deck. He looked up.

'Why! It's the mate.'

'What!' shouted the captain. 'Oh, no!' The men gazed at Jim. They could not forgive him for being in the boat. They all thought that it was George who had come with them.

'What are you doing here? You are a fine one—wouldn't help us—but you came out of your dream in time to save yourself didn't you? In time to save your own rotten life. You're not fit to live.' On and on they went, cursing at him.

'You're not wanted here. What did you do with George?'

'You killed him—you killed him!' shouted one man.

'No!' cried Jim. He realised that these men were now his enemies. Here he was, at their mercy, trapped in a small boat in the open sea; anything could happen to him and no one would ever know.

He sat by himself at one end of the boat. He picked up a piece of wood that he found lying in the bottom of the boat and held it in his hand. He thought, 'If they attack me I can defend myself.'

There he stayed for the rest of that terrible night.

10

The next morning the sea was calm. Jim looked all round at the empty horizon with the eye of a sailor, and he knew that it would be a hot and cloudless day. How lonely the ocean looked, and how tiny they seemed in this endless circle of sea. He looked back into the boat. 'There they sit,' he thought. 'There they sit, the three of them, like dirty old homeless dogs, gazing at me.'

They called to him, 'Come and sit with us, we won't hurt you.'

'You'd better join us,' said another. 'Come on. After all, you jumped too, didn't you?'

The captain said, 'Now we must plan what story to tell, because we must all say the same thing. With any luck, I think we shall see a ship before sunset.'

'I will listen to you from where I am, I don't care what story you invent.'

He thought miserably, 'Nothing they can make people believe will change anything for me. I know what happened. We are cowards—I am a coward—I am no better than any of them. Nothing can change that.'

'Leave him,' said the engineer.

'Oh, he understands well enough. Leave him alone. He'll be all right. What harm can he do us?'

The three men spread the sail over the boat to make a shelter from the sun.

'Keep a look out,' they said to Jim. And to his great satisfaction he saw them all creep under the sail and out of his sight.

The captain's guess was to prove right when, later that day, they saw a ship coming straight towards them. They only had to sit and wait for it, and as it came closer they saw the name on the side of it: Avondale.

The Avondale picked them up, and her captain listened to their story. If any of the men on the Avondale thought that there was something wrong with it, they did not talk about it. Every sailor knows that the captain is the last man to leave a sinking ship; he stays until everyone else is in the boats. So they must have known that it was very unusual to find only one boat, and in it three officers with their captain.

The voyage in the Avondale took ten days, and when they landed the four men were taken to a sailors' home.

But here the most terrible shock was waiting for them. A port officer came to see the captain.

He said, 'Your ship, the Patna, has been brought into the port of Aden by a French warship.'

'But that is impossible!' said the captain. 'We saw her sink.'

'There will be an enquiry,' they were told, 'You will all stay here until the day of the enquiry.'

The captain of the Patna and the two engineers sat quite speechless. This is something that they had not thought about. It did not seem possible. They said nothing. There was nothing to say. The captain of the warship had sent in his report; it was made public; and now everyone knew this strange and puzzling story.

Jim's poor heart lifted a little. Since leaving the Patna and all those people to their fate, in his imagination he had heard cries for help from the sinking ship. Every day, in his guilty heart, he had heard these sounds, and he wondered how long he could bear it before he went mad. Now—he was free of these thoughts, and his only feeling was of happiness that all those people in the Patna were not dead.

'Oh! I'm glad,' he thought. 'However bad my punishment is, I can only feel great joy now that I know that those poor people are safe.' Then he thought. 'What a chance missed! If only I had stayed with the Patna! The one mad moment that made me jump—I've ruined my life.—How dreadful everything will be now. Never again will I be able to look anyone in the face without shame. I wish I were dead.'

11

JIM STANDS ALONE

The captain of the Patna still sat looking in front of him. He couldn't believe that this impossible thing had happened to him. At last he got up and hurried off to the port office, where he had to make a report of the events on the Patna. He was received at once by Captain Elliot, the man in charge of the harbour.

Elliot had a temper, and he could shout. He didn't mind who he shouted at. He always said, 'I'm an old man, and I have always said what I thought.' Now he looked at the captain and hated what he saw.

'You have lied to everyone,' he said. 'You are a coward. Now you must face an enquiry, and what hope is there for you, you worthless fellow? Now get out of my sight. Your report on the Patna hasn't a word of truth in it.'

The captain left the building. Outside, the two engineers and Jim were waiting for him.

'That mad old fool called me worthless!' he said. 'Bah! What do I care? The Pacific Ocean is big—you Englishmen can do your worst. I know there are plenty of other jobs for me. You are all so concerned over this small matter. Well—let them take away my rank—I don't want it—I don't need papers!'

The two engineers looked at each other and laughed. He started to speak again and then changed his mind. He looked about him and saw a horse and carriage a little way off, waiting to be hired. He ran towards it and pushed his way into the carriage.

'Come on!' he shouted to the driver. 'Move! Drive fast, anywhere.' The driver got his horse moving quickly, and off they went. Where? Who knows? They never saw him again. Jim watched his captain disappear out of his life for ever, and he was not at all sorry to see him go.

It so happened that Jim was the only one of the four men who had left the Patna to face the enquiry as a man who had deserted his ship. The engineer with a broken arm was taken to hospital, where he became too ill to attend the enquiry, and the chief engineer spent three days drinking hard, which in the end drove him quite mad for ever more.

12

THE ENQUIRY

Most of the sailors who were in the port at that time attended the enquiry. One of them was a Captain Marlow, owner of several ships in the Pacific. He had nearly reached an age which he considered would be the right time to retire from working and go and spend his last years at home in England. He was an important man

and well known to everybody in the East.

Another man who was sitting next to Marlow at the enquiry said, 'Why are we giving this young man such a bad time?'

Marlow said, 'I really don't know. Why doesn't he just go away? His cowardly captain has gone. Why does he stay? His life as an officer is over anyway, so why stop just to take punishment. No one would stop him if he went.'

'Well,' said the other man, 'I'd say let him creep twenty feet under the ground and stay there!'

'It shows great courage to stay,' said Marlow.

'Courage! That sort of courage is no good. Listen. If you will put down some money, I'll double it and we'll give it to the young fellow to get away. He is an Englishman, after all; it's not right, and all so public, it is very bad.'

Marlow shook his head. 'No, the enquiry must go on,' he said.

Jim interested Marlow very much. He sat and watched as Jim told his story to the judge. Once or twice their eyes met, and each time Jim looked quickly away. He was suspicious of everyone. In his misfortune he could only think that everyone was against him. He could not suppose that anybody would want to be a friend.

At the end of the day, when they were leaving the court, Marlow waited for Jim. But when they met, it was Jim who spoke first, and he was angry.

'What do you mean by looking at me all day?' He stepped nearer to Marlow, who thought he was going to hit him.

'No—stop,' said Marlow. 'I certainly don't want to annoy you. I want to help you.'

Jim moved away quickly without saying a word.

Marlow hurried after him, saying: 'You are running away from me!'

'Never!' shouted Jim, still walking away.

And Marlow realised that his words were the worst he could have used to a poor boy who was being accused at the enquiry of running away. He said, 'I'm sorry. What a stupid thing to say!'

Jim stopped walking then. 'All right,' he said. 'My fault, but I just can't bear all these people looking at me.'

'You need a friend. I can help you. Come and have some dinner with me and we can at least talk about things.'

And to Marlow's surprise Jim agreed to come with him.

13

ALL OVER

After they had eaten, Marlow and Jim went and sat down to talk. Captain Marlow wanted to hear Jim's story; he felt a great interest in the young man.

Jim said, 'I couldn't run away from the enquiry like the others did. My father, poor old man, he will have seen it in all the newspapers by now. I can never face him again. I can never explain to him; he wouldn't understand.'

Marlow said nothing. He wanted Jim to talk.

'What shall I do when this stupid enquiry is finished? I'll never ask for help from home. Perhaps I could get a job as a common sailor?'

Then Marlow spoke. 'Do you think you would? I don't think so. I would like to help you. I saw how you behaved at the enquiry; you were the only one who did not run away from that. I trust you. I know a man in Rangoon who would employ you if I asked him to. I would lend you money—'

'Couldn't think of it,' said Jim.

'I don't expect you to be grateful—you could give back the money when it suited you.'

'Very kind of you,' murmured Jim.

'Well—at least try to tell me what you will do when the enquiry's over.'

'I suppose I'll just go to the devil,' he answered in a low voice.

'Please remember,' said Marlow, 'that I should really like to see you before you decide to do anything.'

'I don't know what's to stop you,' Jim said rudely. 'I'm not likely to disappear—no such luck!'

'Well,' said poor Marlow, 'it's late. I had no idea it was so late.'

Jim got up to go. He shook hands with Marlow and went out quickly. Marlow heard him running down the street.

'Poor boy—not yet twenty-four—running—but with nowhere to go.'

The next day, the second day of the enquiry, Marlow went to the court again.

As he sat there, waiting for the second day of the enquiry to start, he thought, 'This boy has had his punishment: the shame of finding out that he is a coward. No punishment given by the court can be as bad as that.'

The facts given in court that day showed that the Patna was not fit to go to sea. She should never have been allowed to sail.

The next point was the exact cause of the accident. While they were discussing this, the man sitting next to Marlow said,

'It could have been some wreck of a ship floating upside

down just in the path of the Patna—you know—the thing that hit the Patna.'

'Yes, indeed,' answered Marlow, 'that was probably the cause of the accident.' He looked at Jim and saw that he was listening with all his attention to the words being spoken in the court.

At the end of the enquiry the judge said, 'These men are guilty. They will have their rank of officer taken away from them.'

So now Jim knew the worst. It was all over. He rushed out of the court room. Marlow followed him quickly. He came up to Jim and took his arm, but Jim shook himself free.

Marlow stopped and watched him walk away. 'Time enough,' he thought. 'I will find him and talk to him later, when he has been alone for a time.'

14

A NEW START

It was late in the evening when Marlow found Jim down by the water side at the harbour. He saw at once that Jim was in a terrible state. He seemed to be completely confused.

'Come with me,' said Marlow gently.

Jim followed him as quietly as a child. He did not say a word, but perhaps he was pleased that he was not alone any more.

Marlow took him to his room in the hotel where he was staying, so that he could be alone.

'Don't talk,' said Marlow. 'Just sit here and be quiet for a time—it will help you.'

Then Marlow went and sat at his desk. He did not talk, nor did he look at Jim, but started quietly to write some letters.

For a long time Jim seemed to be fighting his despair, trying to find control of himself. He was alone with this kind man, who mercifully took no notice of him. He wept, and he felt that his loneliness was impossible to bear.

Marlow heard him but did not stop writing. He thought, 'How thankful I am that his family do not have to see him in this state. Even I find it hard.'

Then, at last, after a long time, Jim spoke. 'May I have a cigarette?'

Marlow lifted his head and rejoiced. He saw that Jim had got over his storm of despair. 'Yes, of course you may. Take one from that box.'

Jim said. 'That's over! Now it's over, I feel better.' He smiled at Marlow. 'Thank you—your room—it was kind of you. I had nowhere to go. I felt it was the end of everything, but I must go now.' And he got up and walked to the door.

'No, no. Wait!' Marlow cried. 'I must talk to you. I can help you.'

Jim shook his head, 'No one can.'

'Shut the door and come and sit down.'

Jim paused, and then came back into the room. He sat down quietly to listen to what Marlow had to say.

'This is a bad time for you, but I can help you. Let me show you a way out of your despair and loneliness. First of all you must eat. You say that you will not accept the pay for your time on the Patna?'

'No,' said Jim, 'I couldn't do that.'

'Well then, let me tell you my plan. Look at this letter I have written. I want you to take it to a friend of mine. I'm telling him that I trust you—that's what I'm doing.

I have asked him to give you work, and I told him that you are a friend of mine.'

Jim lifted his head. 'Oh!' he said, 'it's wonderfully kind of you!' He jumped up, his eyes shining, 'You are too good!' He shook Marlow's hand and then let it drop at once. 'Why! This is just what I need. It would be very unfriendly of me to refuse. You're splendid! You have helped me—the very thing—the very thing!' and Jim looked at Marlow in surprise and admiration. He walked up and down the room. 'I don't know how to thank you. —There isn't anything I can say. Last night, too. Already you've done me so much good—listening to me, you know.' He stood still in the middle of the room. 'You've given me hope.'

Marlow said, 'Oh for heaven's sake, my dear man—don't!'

'All right, I won't go on. But I've always thought that if a fellow can begin with a new start—and now, you—yes, a fresh beginning!'

Marlow waved his hand in goodbye to this new excited Jim, and Jim marched out, his head held high.

When he had gone, Marlow sighed. 'A new start,' he said to himself. 'Does he not know that our fate is written for us the moment we begin our lives?'

15

ONE CHANCE IN A HUNDRED

Marlow's friend read the letter that Jim brought to him, and was pleased to give Jim work immediately in his rice mill.

This old man lived alone, and usually he did not like

people. He found Jim a pleasant young man, and after Jim had been there a few weeks he asked him to come and live in his house. He was a lonely old man, and Jim's kindness and good manners pleased him very much. He became fond of Jim. Sometimes at meal times he would look at the young man and think:

'Just the sort of boy that I would like for a son. Well, if he continues to take an interest in the work, perhaps I will leave him the rice mill. Then, when I die, he will have it for his own.'

Trouble came suddenly, terrible trouble. Jim could never have guessed that fate could bring such a cruel blow. It was one unlucky chance in a hundred.

One day a man came to the rice mill to look for work, and was given a job of looking after the machinery in the workshop. It was the second engineer of the Patna. Of course the engineer kept silent about the Patna, but Jim could not bear the thought of seeing him every day— reminding him all the time of his failure and of his shameful past.

'The only thing to do is to get away at once,' he thought. 'I cannot deceive my kind employer, I am too fond of him.'

He did not even have the courage to speak to his employer face to face. He wrote him a note and left it on the breakfast table. It said, 'I am sorry I have to leave you at once. I cannot explain why.'

The old man wrote to Marlow. 'Please do not send me any more of your mysterious young men. I shall never try to be kind to anyone again. I was very fond of the boy, and you must know that I am very disappointed.'

16

JIM TRAVELS ON AGAIN

Jim felt he must get a long way from anyone who knew him, and try once again to make a new start.

He went to Bangkok. There he found work quite soon with two men called Egstrom and Blake. They had a store and supplied food and other stores to the ships that came into the port. It was Jim's job to sail a small boat out to the ships before they reached the port and to be the first one to offer the services of his employers. He would go on board and persuade the captain of the ship to buy stores from Egstrom and Blake.

Marlow was on his way to Bangkok in one of his ships when he heard the news that Jim was there. When he arrived, he went to Egstrom and Blake and found Jim. He had just returned from one of his sailing trips.

Marlow said to him, 'Why did you run away from the rice mill?

Jim said, 'It was just as I wrote to you.'

'Well,' said Marlow, 'but why leave? Did the engineer talk?'

'Oh no — he didn't — he made it a sort of secret between us. He used to smile and make secret signs to me and all that sort of thing. One day he even said, "Well this is better than the old ship, isn't it? But don't be afraid — I won't say anything. You just see that I keep my job, and we'll have no quarrel. I've had a hard time since the Patna." It was so hateful — I couldn't stay. I just had to get away.'

Just then Egstrom called from his office, 'There's a ship

coming in, Jim. Away you go.' Marlow shook hands with Jim and turned to go. At the door he looked back at him. 'You know — you have thrown away something like a fortune. That old man was ready to treat you like a son. He was going to leave you all his wealth when he died.'

Jim said, 'I know — I know. Such a splendid old fellow! But what could I do?'

Marlow shook his head in despair.

The next time Marlow's ship called in at Bangkok, he went straight up to Egstrom and Blake to see Jim, but he was unlucky.

'Oh,' said his employer, 'he has left us. He treated us badly, I must say.'

'Where has he gone to? Do you know?' asked Marlow.

'No. And it's no use asking. A man like that doesn't go anywhere in particular.'

Marlow guessed the reason. 'Did anyone talk about a ship called the Patna?'

Egstrom looked surprised. 'Why, yes,' he said. 'That's right, there was a man who came in one day; several of them were talking about the Patna's last voyage. Yes, yes, I remember, that was the day Jim left. He just got up from his dinner — left half of it on the plate too. He just went without a word. One can't get a man like that every day, you know, sir. He was a real devil for a sailing boat — ready to go miles out to sea to meet ships in any sort of weather. More than once a captain has come in here to tell me, "That's a wild kind of madman you employ, Egstrom. Came flying out of the mist this morning right up to my ship's side. I never saw a boat handled like that in my life. Couldn't have been drunk — could he? Such a quiet, polite fellow too, when he came on board." I tell you, Captain Marlow, Jim got us a lot of trade while he was here. And then — suddenly he's gone!'

'He was a mate of the Patna on that last voyage,' said Marlow.

Egstrom looked astonished. Then he said, 'And who on earth cares about that?'

'No one except Jim, I dare say,' Marlow said.

17

MORE TROUBLE FOR JIM

The only luck that poor Jim seemed to have, as he wandered from port to port, was that he got good jobs wherever he went. That is what happened in a small port in Malaysia.

Here he managed to live peacefully for six months before trouble came to him once again.

In the hotel where he lived, he was playing cards with an officer from a warship one evening. The officer was losing every game and was getting angry — he did not like to be beaten. He was drinking a lot and he wanted to start a quarrel. He suddenly laughed at Jim and said,

'You think we don't know who you are. Well then, let me tell you, everybody in the place knows!'

Jim jumped up from his chair full of anger. It was very lucky for the officer that he could swim. The room that they were sitting in opened out on to a narrow path and beyond that a river flowed very wide and black in the night. Before the officer could defend himself, Jim picked him up and threw him into the river. It was lucky for the officer that a boat load of Chinese were passing up the river. Hearing the sound of something big falling into the water, they looked about them. They saw him and fished him out of the water.

Once again Captain Marlow was there to help. Jim arrived on his ship at about midnight. He had run out of the hotel, hatless and in despair.

'Every man in the place knows my secret! Here I thought I was safe, but all the time they knew! I can't go back there. Take me away with you!'

In the morning the owner of the hotel explained to Marlow that he could not have Jim there to live any more.

'No, no! A temper like that won't do. He is a nice enough young fellow, but the officer he treated so roughly is nice too.'

So Marlow took Jim away with him when he sailed. The ship was at sea for a long time. Jim's behaviour made Marlow very sad. He stayed by himself, and though he was a seaman he took less interest in the ship than an ordinary passenger. He stayed below decks like an escaped prisoner.

Captain Marlow tried to talk to him. He said, 'Would you like to leave this part of the world? Try California or the West Coast? I'll see what I can do.'

But Jim said, 'What difference would it make?'

And Marlow thought to himself, 'He is probably right. I have given him many chances, but not the right one — surely there is something — but what more can I do?' And he remembered once again the man sitting next to him at the Patna enquiry, and what he said, 'Let him creep twenty feet underground and stay there!'

18

MARLOW GOES TO SEE STEIN

After some weeks they arrived at a port. Marlow felt he must try once again to do something to help Jim. He wanted to help him, and he still had faith in him, so he did not give up hope that something could be done to give him a fresh start.

He decided to go and see a good friend who lived quite near. This friend was a wealthy and respected merchant. His name was Stein. Marlow was anxious to seek his advice. Stein was one of the most trustworthy men he had ever known, and he knew that he could explain his difficulty to him.

It was evening when Marlow reached Stein's house. He was led into a large dimly lit room by a Javanese servant.

Stein turned round in his chair, pushing his eyeglasses up on his head, and greeted Marlow with warmth. He was a gentle man of about sixty, and his great interest in life besides his work was many hundreds of insects which he had collected over the years from the many countries he had visited.

'Sit down,' he said. 'And what is your good news?'

'To tell you the truth, Stein,' said Marlow, 'I have come here to ask your advice about a man.'

Stein looked at him for a moment. 'Well,' he said, 'I am a man too.'

Marlow told him all about Jim. When he had finished, Stein uncrossed his legs, laid down his pipe, leaned forwards with his arms on the sides of his chair, the tips of his fingers together. He said, 'I understand very well. He is a dreamer.'

'You are right. That's exactly what he is. How simple you make it sound! But what's good for it?'

'There is only one cure for it, and that must come from the person himself.'

Marlow said, 'Yes, but really the question is not how to get cured, but how to live!'

Stein nodded his head sadly. 'It's not good for you to find you cannot make your dream come true because you are not strong enough or clever enough.' Then Stein got up from his chair and said, 'It's late. Tonight you sleep here, and in the morning we shall think of something. He is a dreamer, and that is bad — very bad. But perhaps very good too.'

It was at the breakfast table the next morning that Stein mentioned Patusan.

'I don't know the place,' said Marlow.

'No. Not many people do. It is a small place, some miles up a river, very far from any other village. I have a trading post there, and I want a manager for it. I wonder if your young friend would consider going there. He would have to live in Patusan. It would be a lonely sort of job, far away from everybody. He would be the only white man there. There is a man named Cornelius there now, but he is no good, and it is time there was a change. Do you think Jim would like to come and see me about it?'

'I will go and ask him,' said Marlow. 'It seems to me that it would be a great chance for him. I am indeed grateful to you for being willing to give this boy a chance. I trust him and I believe this may be the right thing for him.'

19

'I'LL NEVER GO HOME AGAIN'

He found Jim, as usual, below decks and said to him,
'I don't suppose you have ever heard of Patusan?'

'Never,' said Jim.

'No. Not many people have. It is a small and very
lonely place, about forty miles away from the sea, up a
river which is also called Patusan. There is a trading post
in the village belonging to my friend Stein, and he is
willing to offer you a job as manager there.'

'Bury me there, would you? cried Jim.

'No, no,' said Marlow. 'It could be a wonderful new
start in life for you. The new manager must be a man of
character and honesty, with a strong will to lead the
people under him.'

Jim looked ashamed. 'You are so kind to me that I
ought to be grateful, and, indeed, I am most grateful. I
can't think why you haven't stopped trying to help me
long ago.'

'Well, then, if you wish to show that you are grateful,
please go and see Stein and talk to him.'

'I'll go. I know now that I'll never go home again. I
must make some sort of a life for myself. If it is to be in
Patusan — well, then — I must try it.'

And so Jim went to see Stein. He did not return until
the next morning. Stein asked him to stay for dinner and
for the night. Stein had liked Jim from the first moment
that he saw him.

'You are young and strong; but I think I must tell you
what sort of place this Patusan is. It is a country that is

ruled by its own people, and sometimes they do not allow strangers or foreigners up the river to their village. I have had no news from there for twelve months. My manager is called Cornelius. I am not at all pleased with his work. He cheats me and steals from me, and if you decide to go there I would like you to take his place. There is much to be put right. You will have enemies, and the *Raja*, who is the ruler, will try to kill you, I have no doubt about that. But it is a great chance for someone young like you to succeed. Do you think it is the sort of thing that you would like to take a risk for, and try it?'

Jim said, 'More than anything!' He felt his heart lifting. He thought, 'Could this be my chance at last? Can I now prove to myself that I am worth something?'

'I don't know why you should want to go to such a place,' said Stein. 'However, Marlow has sent you to me, and that makes it all right as far as I am concerned.'

Jim looked down at the floor. 'I will do everything I can to make a success of my work there, and you can trust me.'

'Yes, I think I can. Well — this Raja Allang, the ruler of the place, treats people badly. He robs other villages, even many miles away. It is a rule of terror. The poor people can do nothing. They cannot get away from him. Where would they go? They want a strong man who would lead them, who could give them some power to defend themselves. Then, perhaps, there would be peace and order once more.'

20

THE SILVER RING

The next morning Stein gave Jim a letter for Cornelius and said, 'He must tell you about the work, and then he must give you control of everything.'

Then Stein took something out of his pocket and said, 'This ring was given to me as a sign of friendship by a man in Patusan called Doramin. He is a very good friend of mine. He fights the Raja as well as he can for more justice for the people. If you ever need a friend or are in danger, take this ring to Doramin. He will know where it came from, and I have no doubt that he will help you in every possible way.'

Jim took the ring and looked at it. Already it meant a sign of trust and friendship. His hand closed over it. He held it as if it was treasure.

He thought, 'It is like something you read of in books. It is what I have been waiting for! Now I am ready for anything. I will face danger! I will show what I am made of! A chance to get out of this — shut the door — shut out the world — this is surely luck at last!'

He left Stein's house and returned to Marlow's ship with the news.

'Now,' he said to Marlow, 'this is my chance. I can forget the past, forget the world. And the world can forget me, at last. But I shall never forget you!'

'It is not I, or the world who remember,' Marlow shouted at him. 'It is you — you who remember.'

Then, more quietly, he said, 'Well, forget me too if it would help. But one day you will want to come back.'

'Come back to what?'

Marlow sat silent for a moment. Then he said, 'It is to be never, then?'

'Never!' said Jim. 'And now I must go back to Stein and get my final orders. There is a boat sailing for Patusan this afternoon.'

'You are going so soon then?' They took each other's hands and exchanged last hurried words. Marlow felt closer to Jim than ever before.

'Take care of yourself. Don't take risks.'

'All right, all right!' said Jim. He wanted to say some grateful words, to try to thank Marlow for everything that he had done for him. 'I promise to take care. Not a single blessed risk. Don't you worry. — Jove! I feel as if nothing can touch me. — I couldn't spoil such a chance!'

21

PATUSAN, JIM'S NEW HOME

The ship that was taking Jim to Patusan stopped at the mouth of the river. The captain would not go any further.

'The last time I went up this river,' he said, 'I was fired on from the forest on both banks of the river, and then my ship was nearly wrecked on a sandbank.'

They saw a small boat rowing towards them. It had come from a village on the river bank. There were three men in it. They were willing to take Jim up the river to Patusan.

Jim sat in the little boat, feeling very lonely, as it moved away from the ship. He was really starting on his new adventure now.

'I could be disappearing from the earth, and leaving

no trace,' he thought.

It was a long hot journey, there was no shelter from the hot sun streaming down on him, and at times he felt faint with weariness in the heat.

At last, suddenly, at a bend in the river the first houses of Patusan came into sight. Rising up from the level of the water, there were two steep hills very close together. The river, narrow and deep at this place, flowed between them.

The men in the boat rowed to a low point of land and jumped out and ran away. Jim at once took a great leap out of the boat and ran after them. A lot of people were coming towards him and shouting. Jim looked back and saw a boat full of armed men on the river, cutting off any possible escape for him.

Jim stood still. As the people came up to him, he said, 'What is the matter?'

'The Raja wants to see you,' said one of them.

'All right,' said Jim. 'Here I am!'

They took his luggage away from him and then searched him and took an unloaded pistol that he was carrying. Then they pushed him roughly in front of them all the way to the Raja's house.

He was taken to a very dirty courtyard. There he remained as a prisoner for three days. He had very little to eat, just a small amount of rice and some fish. During this time the Raja and his advisers could not decide what they should do with him. Usually they killed their prisoners at once, but they were not sure where Jim had come from, and they were afraid that someone might come and punish them if they harmed him.

After three days, Jim decided that he had spent long enough in these dreadful conditions. He made up his mind to escape. Stein had described to him where

Doramin, his friend, lived, and Jim thought the time had come to show Doramin the ring and ask for his help.

There was a weak place in the fence which surrounded him. Jim walked away from this to the far side of the courtyard. Then he turned quickly and ran as fast as he could towards the weak place, took a great flying leap, and broke through it. He landed in the soft mud of the river. It was lucky for him that the tide was out and there was no water there, but he sank deeply into the mud. He struggled to free himself and lay full length tearing at the mud with his hands, and trying to pull and push himself along.

At last he reached the edge of the mud, on the other side of the river bed. He lay for a time, too worn out to move, and almost wishing that he had not started on this dangerous journey, and that he was safely back in his prison.

'I must get on. They will find out that I have gone, and will follow me,' he thought. At last he got his breath back and started to run. He was covered in wet black mud. He came to a village, and some children ran away from him crying, frightened by this muddy creature running so fast — a flying terror.

'Doramin!' Jim shouted, hoping that someone would help him. He felt sure that his enemies must be close behind him. Then he almost ran into two men, who looked very surprised at the sight of this stranger covered in mud.

'Doramin, Doramin,' he whispered with his last breath. The two men held him up, and half-carried him to Doramin.

22

DORAMIN

There was great excitement among the people as Jim was half-carried to the top of a slope and into a garden full of fruit trees. Here there was a very large man sitting in a chair, and Jim's helpers stopped in front of him. He felt about in his muddy clothes to find his precious ring, but suddenly he found himself lying on his back. He wondered who had knocked him down. The two men had stopped holding him up, and he was too weak to stand alone. He heard shots being fired at the bottom of the slope, but he was safe. Doramin's people were shutting the gates which guarded the village, and the Raja's men would not come any further looking for their prisoner.

Water was poured down Jim's throat, and then Doramin's old wife ordered her servants to take him to bed, where he just lay, unable to move for a long time.

Doramin was the chief of the second power in Patusan. He ruled about sixty families, and about two hundred men formed his small army. With these he defended his people against the Raja, who robbed and killed in all the defenceless villages.

The quarrels between the two powers were usually about trading, and fighting would start, and the villages would be filled with smoke and flame, cries of pain and fear, and the noise of shots being fired. Whole villages were often burnt to the ground, and men were dragged into the Raja's land to be killed or cruelly *tortured* for the crime of trading with anybody besides the Raja himself.

To make matters much worse, just recently another

group of men were gathered together into a rough sort of army by a wandering Arab called Sherif Ali. He made a fortress on the top of one of the two hills. He also attacked the villages, stealing from the people.

Some of Doramin's men wanted to join with Sherif Ali, so that they would be stronger to fight against the hated Raja Allang. The younger men, particularly, said, 'Get Sherif Ali and his wild men to help us to drive Raja Allang out of the country.'

Doramin would not agree to this plan.

When Jim was feeling stronger, and was able to stand and walk by himself again, he was taken to see Doramin once more.

He said, 'Stein sent me to Patusan to be his manager at his trading post. I am to take the place of Cornelius. As soon as I arrived, and landed from my boat, I was taken by the Raja's men and put into his prison yard. I escaped from there, and have come to you for help. This ring will make it clear to you that I come from Stein. He told me that you had given it to him in friendship, and he said that if I ever needed help you would give it to me.'

Doramin looked very pleased. 'My friend Stein, yes— yes, I gave him the ring. Of course you must stay here, and we will plan how to get you safely to the trading post.'

Jim liked Doramin immediately and felt his courage returning. He had found friends in this strange and frightening country.

Doramin was a very grand old man. He was taller than most of his men and very large and fat. He could not move without the help of two boys who stayed on each side of him. When he wanted to get up, he used to turn his head slowly to the right, and then to the left, and they helped him up.

In the days that followed, Jim learnt a great deal about the history of Patusan, and about the very troubled times that had come to this unknown part of Malaysia. He became very friendly with Doramin's greatly loved only son, Dain Waris. The two of them spent many hours together, talking and planning to bring peace to the country.

'First,' said Jim, 'I must go back and find Cornelius and start doing the work that Stein has sent me to do. I will return to you as soon as possible. I want to help you to fight Sherif Ali. Together, with your people, we will stop the killing and the attacks that keep us all in a state of fear.'

'It is too soon for you to go back,' said Dain Waris. 'The Raja will find you, and he will certainly kill you this time.'

'I must take the risk of that happening. It is my duty to go. I am Stein's manager.'

'Well, if you must, go, but come back if you want help.'

Jim said, 'You are my friends. I can never forget your kindness. One day I hope to show you how grateful I am.'

23

'WHY DO YOU LET HIM DO IT?'

And so Jim came to the house where Cornelius lived. He was not happy when he saw the house. It was dirty, and the roof had fallen down in some places. Jim thought that Cornelius was a dreadful little man, and he made up his mind that he would stay there for only a short time. But he said to Cornelius, 'Stein has told me that I must live in your house until I can build one of my own.'

'Yes, yes, certainly,' said Cornelius, trying very hard to be pleasant. 'But you cannot expect to stay for nothing. —Stein would not expect me to keep you for nothing. You must pay me.'

Jim soon found out that Cornelius was not honest. Stein was right when he said that Cornelius cheated him. The man had cheated Stein from the first.

Cornelius's second wife's daughter also lived in the house with him. Her mother had married Cornelius after the girl's father had died. Now her mother was also dead. Cornelius kept the girl with him, but he was very unkind to her all the time.

He said, 'I keep you here. It costs me money. And why do I keep you? Out of the kindness of my heart.— And are you grateful? Do you call me father? No, never!'

The girl hated him. Jim thought she led a terrible life. She was very beautiful, and sometimes when Cornelius was shouting at her, Jim could not bear it and walked out of the room.

He said to her one day, 'Why do you let him do it? Just give me permission, and I'll punish him for treating you so badly.'

The girl said, 'If he was not such a miserable old man, I would kill him with my bare hands!'

Jim was shocked that a young girl should have such thoughts; but as time passed, he began to have his own reasons for wishing that Cornelius was out of the way. He realised that Cornelius hated him and was planning to have him sent away from Patusan for ever.

Indeed Cornelius hated the young man who had been sent to take his place. First he tried to frighten Jim away.

He said to him, 'The Raja will kill you; he can't forgive you for escaping from his prison. I can get you taken down the river and right away from Patusan if you will give me eighty dollars; such a small amount to save you; see what a good friend I am to you!'

'No!' shouted Jim. 'I am going to live in Patusan. I have a job to do and you cannot stop me.'

'You will die here,' whispered Cornelius.

A few days after this quarrel with Cornelius, Jim decided that it was time to go to see Doramin again. He had a plan in his mind to fight and conquer Sherif Ali, to destroy him for ever and bring peace to Patusan. He felt strongly that he had power to save these people.

Cornelius watched him get ready to leave. 'But I suppose you will come back to my poor house?' he murmured. Jim nodded but did not look at him. He hated this nasty old man, and he hated the secret way he crept about and watched every movement that Jim made.

And so Jim went back to his friends. He spent the day with Doramin and Dain Waris, planning Sherif Ali's destruction.

Doramin was doubtful that they could send a force to the top of the hill where Sherif Ali had his fortress.

'Sherif Ali must be beaten,' said Jim.

'But how?' asked Doramin. 'He lives at the top of that hill where no one can reach him.'

Jim remembered his journey up the river, and his first sight of Patusan with its two hills standing up so close together, only a narrow valley separating them.

He said, 'You have two guns on wheels. I have seen them. If we could push the guns to the top of your hill, you could fire across the valley and hit his hill. You could destroy his fort. Then your men could be waiting at the foot of his hill to climb up and destroy Sherif Ali's force. They would be taken by surprise by the attack, their fort would be in ruins, and it would be easy to beat them.'

Dain Waris's dark eyes shone. He looked at Jim, and

knew that here was a man who could lead them—a man they could trust. He said, 'Let us go up to the top of our hill at once. Let me see how your plan would work! This is our chance, father, a wonderful chance!'

Doramin at last agreed that the plan was a possible one and had a good chance of success.

Jim returned to Cornelius's house that night, well pleased with the day's work, and knowing that he would return soon to lead Doramin's men into battle with his own plan to destroy Sherif Ali. By doing that, he would also put fear into Raja Allang's heart.

24

THE GIRL AND JIM

That night Jim woke suddenly; there was a light in his room, and there was somebody there.

'Get up! Get up! Get up!' He leapt to his feet quickly. He recognised the girl. She was holding a flaming light in her hand. She put his pistol into his hand. He held it in silence, blinded by the light and wondering what he could do to help her.

She whispered, 'Can you face four men?'

'Certainly—of course—glad to help you.' He was still only half awake, but he wished to be properly polite to her.

'Follow me,' she said.

They went through the house. 'They were going to kill you while you slept,' she said quietly.

Jim was suddenly angry. People were always coming up to him and telling him he was going to be killed. 'I thought you needed my help,' he said, and turned to go back to bed.

'No, no! Follow me!'

Jim said, 'If there is danger, you should not be here. Will you go back and send my servant Tamb' Itam to me.'

'There is no time. They are in the shed, waiting in hiding, they are waiting for a sign,' she said.

'Who is to give the sign?' he asked. But he knew the answer. It would be Cornelius who was working against him again, and he was probably being paid by Sherif Ali.

'I have been watching each night beside your bed. You think I have only watched tonight?'

Jim felt as if he had received a blow in his chest. He felt *touched*—sorry and happy all at once. That this beautiful girl should feel so concerned for him was indeed a wonderful surprise.

Suddenly she said, 'Wait here, until you hear my voice.' And she ran ahead of him with her flaming *torch*.

He waited outside the door of the shed. Not a sound came from inside it.

Then he heard her call, 'Now! Open the door!' He pushed the door with all his strength and came into a dark room. The girl held the torch through the window, and smoke and flame filled the room. He saw her bare arm stretched through the window, holding the light so that he could see into the darkness.

'Fire! Defend yourself!' He heard her words and looked wildly around, and suddenly he saw someone move.

'Come out!' he called angrily. A man jumped out of the shadows. His right arm was raised, ready to strike at Jim with a knife that he held in his hand. Jim watched him coming towards him. He waited. The man took three steps forward. Then Jim fired. He saw the man's head go up, saw him throw his arms forward and drop the knife. He fell to the ground, dead.

Another figure came into sight, but as Jim raised his

gun to fire at him the man threw down his knife.

'You want me to save your life?' asked Jim. 'Then tell me, how many more of you are there?'

'Two more,' said the man in a frightened voice, looking at Jim's gun.

25

JIM KNOWS HE IS IN LOVE

Jim took his prisoners out of the shed. He held his gun ready to fire at them.

'All of you, hold each other's arms,' he said. They obeyed him at once.

'The first one to turn his head is a dead man,' Jim said. 'Now, march!'

They stepped out together, and he followed, and by his side the girl carried the light.

They came to the river bank.

'Stop!' said Jim. The bank was steep, and the light of the torch fell on the smooth water.

'Take my greetings to Sherif Ali—till I come myself,' said Jim. Then, 'Jump!' he shouted.

The water shot up into the air as they all jumped together. Their heads disappeared under the water, and when they came up they were swimming hard, as fast as they could, to get away from this powerful man. They expected a shot to follow them as they went.

Jim turned to the girl. He looked into her eyes for a long time. She suddenly threw the torch away into the river. Then she began to weep. Jim held her in his arms. His heart was full. He had not known how much she cared for him. He was joyful at the thought of her loving

care. It seemed wonderful to him, and he suddenly knew
that he loved her, and now he only wanted to protect
her and take her away from the terrible life she led with
Cornelius.

26

THE END OF SHERIF ALI

Jim knew that the time had now come to fight and
beat Sherif Ali. He returned to Doramin, and he was
very pleased to find that all the men had been called
together to work on the plan to attack the fort on the
opposite hill.

That night, as soon as it was dark, they started to drag
Doramin's two guns up the hill. Jim's sea training was
put to good use. He showed the men how to use ropes
to pull the guns up the hill with a *capstan,* which they
made out of a log of wood standing upright. This had
a rope round it and a thick stick through it, which was
turned by two men. The end of the rope was tied to one
gun and so the capstan was able to take the heavy weight
as the two men slowly turned it. Then with men pushing
behind the gun, it began to move slowly up the hill.

They worked all night. First one gun and then the
other were slowly dragged up the hill. Big fires were
lighted to help them to see, and Jim and Dain Waris
went up and down, directing the work and encouraging
the men.

Doramin was watching. He was carried to a level place
half way up the hill, and there he sat in the light of the
fires, moving neither hand nor foot, watching his people
all around him working and shouting. Sherif Ali must

have thought that they were all mad. He certainly never troubled himself to come out and see what they were doing.

No one would have thought it possible to mount guns on top of the hill, and Jim suspected that these men, working so hard, also did not think that it was possible; but they worked on, and before daylight their task was done. Both guns were in place and ready to fire at Sherif Ali's fort.

At sunrise the guns were fired. Across the valley they saw Sherif Ali's camp on the other hill fall to pieces. There were bits of wood flying everywhere. The enemy was taken completely by surprise, and Jim saw men running in all directions.

'We can do no more here,' he said to Dain Waris. 'Let us join your men who are waiting to attack the hill.'

They ran down to the valley between the hills to lead the men who were waiting to attack and capture the remains of Sherif Ali's camp.

Jim and Dain Waris were the first to reach the fence surrounding the camp. Most of it had been knocked to pieces by the guns. Jim pushed his shoulder against it and it gave way, sending him flying, head first, to the ground inside. One of the enemy ran towards him with a spear and would have killed him if Dain Waris had not been close behind and saved him. The third man through was Tamb' Itam, Jim's servant, a faithful shadow who hardly ever left Jim's side. These three, and the attacking party came in so quickly, with frightening shouts and war cries, that there were cries of anger, surprise and fear from the other side, and in five minutes of fierce fighting it was all over.

The victory was complete. Doramin, waiting in his chair on the hillside, received the news. When he heard that his son was safe, he tried without another sound, to get up. His two boys hurried to help him, and held him respectfully as he walked slowly home.

Jim stayed on the hill, turning his back on the scene of the battle. He looked down on Patusan, and saw the open spaces between the houses fill with people. They had heard the news of the battle. He heard a great noise of drums, and the wild shouts of the people reached his ears.

'My victory!' he whispered to himself. 'At last I have proved my courage.'

27

LORD JIM

Patusan was a joyful village. Jim was suddenly famous. All the people thought that he was a man of strange and great powers. They called him Tuan Jim, which means, in English, Lord Jim.

But the Raja's fear was great. 'I shall be driven from my land by that white devil. My turn will come!'

But, indeed, Lord Jim saved his life. There were many who wanted to continue the war against the Raja, and to punish him for all his cruelty to them. But Jim stopped them doing this. He knew that the Raja would not have the courage to try to rule Patusan after what had happened to Sherif Ali.

Jim was still living in Cornelius's house. He felt that he could not leave the girl there alone; it would be as if he had deserted her. He decided he would build a house for them both as soon as he could.

Cornelius hated him more than ever, and Jim knew

that he was a dangerous enemy; but he also knew that he loved the girl and he would give his life to protect her. He invented the name of Jewel for her because she was so precious to him.

'Nothing can ever make me leave you,' he said.

'But you will go away—they all go—the strangers that come here.'

Jim said, 'I shall never go, I am not like the others, I cannot go.'

'But why?' she asked.

'Because I am not good enough.'

'You lie!'

'No, hear me.' And Jim told Jewel the terrible story of the Patna.

'I cannot believe you,' she said. 'I will never believe that you were afraid. No one would ever believe you. You are the bravest man in all the world. I love you.'

One day Cornelius came to Jim. 'That girl,' he said. 'She is yours, but you ought to give me a present. After all, she is my daughter.'

Jim looked at him; he was puzzled; he did not understand what Cornelius meant.

Cornelius explained: 'Soon you will go back to where you came from, and then I will promise to look after her again. No more trouble for you—just some money now.' His voice was begging. 'Every gentleman provides for when the time comes to go home.'

'In my case,' said Jim, 'the time will never come.'

'What!' shouted Cornelius.

Jim said, 'Haven't you heard me say often enough that this is my home. Jewel will be my wife. I am never going away.'

'You come here from the devil knows where,' shouted Cornelius, 'and the devil knows why—to trouble me until I die—nobody knows why. Ha! We shall see! we shall see! What—steal from me? Everything, everything, everything.' His head bowed. One would think that he loved the girl with a great love and that now his heart was breaking.

Suddenly he lifted his head. 'Like her mother, she is exactly—in her face too—deceiving—the devil.'

Jim left him. He was too annoyed to stay near him any longer. Cornelius shouted after him, 'We shall see. Never leave here? We shall see!'

28

AN UNWELCOME STRANGER

Now that Sherif Ali had gone for ever, the Raja was quiet, but not yet friendly. He was too frightened to annoy Jim in any way; and Jim decided that it was time to build his house and make a safe home for his Jewel while there was peace in Patusan. His house was also to be a fort with water surrounding it. His friend Doramin had agreed to supply him with guns to protect him and his people against anyone who tried to attack them. All his followers in Patusan would be able to come there for safety if in sudden danger. These people, who had mostly been slaves of Sherif Ali, until Jim had made them free, he called his 'own people'. They had their special part of Patusan to live in, which was near Jim's fort.

Jewel was with Jim now. But Cornelius remained his enemy and was always planning to do him some harm.

The trading post was rich, and much business was done now that traders were not afraid to come to Patusan. Stein heard good reports of Jim's work. He wrote to

Marlow: 'We did well to give him a chance. He is doing well and seems content to stay in Patusan for ever.'

For three years after Jim came to Patusan, there was peace. The Raja still did not like Jim, but he was afraid of him and kept very quiet. Cornelius still hated Jim, but nobody took any notice of the poor old man.

Then one day, when Jim was away, trading in a distant village, a stranger arrived in Patusan. His arrival changed everything. His name was Brown. He was a *pirate*, that is a man who sails the seas in an armed ship with criminals as crew. They used to choose a ship that probably had a rich cargo, fire their guns at it to make it stop, and then go on board and take the ship and its cargo for themselves. Sometimes they even killed the captain and the men of the ship. For some strange reason, Brown was known as 'Gentleman Brown' by everyone in the Western Pacific.

But lately he had not been so successful. He had wrecked his ship on some rocks along the coast a few hundred miles from the Patusan river. In a small port he had managed to steal a Spanish ship, and had sailed away one dark night; but he and his men were hungry, they had no food or money.

Brown sailed his stolen ship along the coast until he came to the Patusan river. Here he left her a mile or so out to sea, and took about a dozen of his men in a small boat up the river until they came to the village of Patusan.

When they arrived, Brown was very puzzled to find that Patusan was so big. There was nobody in sight and no one came to greet them. Brown decided to land and try to reach the centre of the village before anyone saw him.

He was not successful; he had been seen coming up the river and a warning had gone round that an un-

friendly-looking boat was approaching.

A shout went up as Brown landed. There was a sound of drums beating all the way up the river. Guns were fired, and Brown's men, feeling trapped, returned the fire. A battle started.

Brown hated these people who had dared to defend themselves. There was no escape now, and all he could do was to return to his boat with his men and row on up the river to a narrow part further up. Here they landed again, and at once started to build themselves some protection, by cutting down trees and bushes and building a wall.

The Raja, who considered himself to be the head of the village while Lord Jim was absent, ordered his men not to attack, but to keep a good watch on these new enemies and make sure that they did not return to the village.

All night Brown expected to be attacked, but he was left alone as if he was already dead.

29

CORNELIUS TAKES HIS CHANCE

Meanwhile, a messenger was sent to Jim to call him back. Doramin wanted his help. He knew that Lord Jim was the one who would have the right answer. He also feared for his son. Dain Waris had been the first to fire on Brown, and Doramin did not want him to continue with the attack. The headmen of the village agreed with this and wanted to wait for Jim's return before any action was taken.

They all met in Jim's fort. Kassim, the Raja's head

man, was also there.

'Father,' said Dain Waris, 'let us attack at once, and kill these men. They are evil.'

'No, son, we must wait,' said Doramin. 'But you will take some boats and some men with weapons, and go down the river to guard it in case these men escape us, and also prevent any more of these evil men coming up the river.'

Doramin thought this plan would keep Dain Waris out of danger, and indeed perhaps save his life.

The Raja was happy. He now thought of a plan to get rid of Jim for ever. He sent Kassim and Cornelius to talk to Brown. Cornelius was ordered to go forward alone, as he could speak English to Brown.

He called out, 'I am a white man. A poor old man who has lived here for years. I want to talk to you.'

Brown answered, 'Come on, then—but come alone!' Cornelius crept up towards Brown.

'Come!' Brown said. 'You are safe.'

This was the chance that Cornelius was waiting for. Here was someone who would listen to him. He started to give Brown a great deal of useful knowledge, and told him that the Raja would support him if he attacked Patusan.

'Food,' said Brown. 'We want food at once.'

Brown was delighted. He had come to steal some food and perhaps some money. Now he saw that with the Raja's help he could take the whole place. This Lord Jim that they talked about had made himself their ruler.

'Why shouldn't I do the same thing?' he thought.

Cornelius had settled in Brown's camp. He told Brown many useful things about Jim and his fort.

Brown said, 'What's his name? Jim? Jim! That's not enough for a man's name.'

Cornelius said, 'They call him Tuan Jim, as you would say, Lord Jim.'

'What is he? Where does he come from?' asked Brown. 'Is he an Englishman?'

'Yes, he is English, and he is a fool. All you need to do is to kill him, and then you are king here. Everything belongs to him.'

'It seems possible that I might be able to make him share everything with me before long,' said Brown.

'No, no. The proper way is to kill him the first chance you get, and then you can do what you like. I have lived here for many years and I am giving you a friend's advice.'

30

JIM RETURNS—TO WHAT?

Dain Waris took his boats and men, armed with guns, and made a camp down the river some distance from Patusan.

And during that day Brown was careful to make Kassim and Cornelius think that he would fight with them against Jim. But what he really planned to do was to talk to Jim. He thought that it would be best to talk business with Jim. He would offer to share. They would be as brothers.

'Until perhaps we have a quarrel,' thought Brown. 'Easy enough to start a quarrel at the right time, then— a shot fired, the end of Lord Jim, a sad business, of course, but I would be there to take his place and rule the people of Patusan.'

So he waited. Kassim must be fooled, so that food would be brought to them.

The next day, very early, there was suddenly a great noise in Patusan. All the lights were being lit, drums were beating and shouts could be heard.

'What's that?' said Brown.

Cornelius answered, 'He has come.'

'What? Lord Jim? Already? Are you sure?'

'Yes, yes sure. Listen to the noise.'

'What are they making all that noise about?'

'For joy,' Cornelius said. 'He is a very great man, but all the same he knows no more than a child, so they make a great noise to please him, because they are like children too.'

'How can I talk to him?' asked Brown.

'He will come here,' said Cornelius.

'What do you mean? Will he just come up here?'

Cornelius nodded. 'Yes, he will come straight here and talk to you. You will see what a fool he is.'

'I don't believe he will come here.'

'You will see, you will see,' Cornelius said again. 'He is not afraid—not afraid of anything. He will come and order you to leave his people alone. Yes, and then you can shoot him. Just kill him, and it will frighten everyone so much that you will be able to do what you like, take what you like. Ha! Ha! Fine!' Cornelius almost danced for joy.

31

A TRAPPED RAT CAN BITE

It was daylight when Brown saw a man coming towards him from the village, and he went to meet him.

He hated Jim at first sight. This was not the man that

he expected to see. He cursed Jim's youth, his clear eyes and his untroubled look. He did not look like a man he could bargain with.

'Who are you?' asked Jim.

'My name is Brown—Captain Brown. What's yours?'

Jim said, 'What made you come here?'

'You want to know? It's easy to tell you. Hunger. And why did you come here?'

Jim looked astonished, and got red in the face.

That pleased Brown. By accident he had found a weak spot in Jim.

'Who is he?' thought Brown. 'He is a mystery. What is he doing here?'

'Let us agree to talk,' said Brown. 'Here I am, like a rat in a trap, but even a trapped rat can bite.'

'Not if you don't go near the trap until the rat has died of hunger.'

'Surely,' said Brown, 'you, as a white man, would not leave us here. Will you not let us out? We are white men, too. Surely you will be on our side?'

Jim said, 'Why should I save you? You don't deserve it. You came here to rob and kill us.'

'And what do you deserve?' asked Brown. 'We came here to ask for food. And you fired your guns at us. You attacked us. Now, we ask: either you fight us or give us a clear road back to our ship.'

'I would fight you now,' said Jim.

'And I could let you shoot me,' said Brown. 'But that would be too easy. I am not the sort to jump out of trouble and leave my men to fight by themselves.'

Jim looked down on the ground. 'How is it,' he said, 'that you are so penniless, and without food?'

But Brown shouted at him, 'Is this the story of our lives? Well, while we are at it, what is it that you have done—something so bad that you have to hide yourself away from everyone? All I ask is to be shot quickly or else to be thrown out and allowed to die in my own way.'

'You killed some of our own men.'

'They attacked us first,' said Brown. 'We came in peace up the river, and they fired at us. I had to protect my men.'

Jim stood there with nothing to say. His eyes showed anger—and something else.

Brown looked at him. He knew that he had said something that had really troubled Jim. He wished that he could guess what it was, so that he could go on attacking Jim with words. He went on talking, hoping to find out something.

'Have you nothing to be ashamed of? Nothing in all your life?'

Jim was forced to remember his cowardly behaviour in the Patna. It was something that he hoped to forget for ever out here, away from the world. He wanted to get rid of this man as quickly as he could.

'Would you give me a promise to leave Patusan peacefully?' Jim asked.

Brown nodded his head. He was unable to believe his luck.

'And,' said Jim, 'leave your guns here?'

'No. Not that. You would have to take them out of our dead hands. You think I am mad? They are the only things I have got that would make a bit of money if I sold them.'

'I will let you go then. But if you use your guns against us we will kill you all. You shall have a clear road or a clear fight.' He turned and walked away.

Cornelius rushed up to Brown. 'Why didn't you kill him?' he asked.

'Because I can do better than that!' answered Brown.

32

TAMB' ITAM IS SHOCKED

Jim went straight to Doramin, who had come over to the fort for talks.

'I have decided that it is best to let the white men go. No more fighting. It is best for our people, Brown has promised to go peacefully.'

'I do not trust this man Brown,' said Doramin. 'He did not come here with the intention of going away with nothing.'

But Jim persuaded him. 'It will be best to let these white people go with their lives. You have always been able to trust me—believe me—I am right.'

He looked at Doramin, but Doramin did not speak.

'Then,' said Jim, 'call in Dain Waris, your son, my friend. If you want to fight, I do not wish to lead our people into such a battle.'

Tamb' Itam, Jim's servant, standing behind Jim's chair, was shocked. His master—his god—refusing to fight. 'How could anyone trust a man like Brown?' he said to himself.

In the end Doramin agreed. But Jewel shook her head in great doubt. Something was wrong. Jim had made a big mistake, she was sure.

'They are bad men,' she said to Jim.

'Men sometimes act badly without being much worse than anyone else.'

Now that Brown was free to go, Jim decided to send Tamb' Itam to tell Dain Waris that the white men were not to be stopped on their way down the river.

Tamb' Itam asked his master for some proof so that Dain Waris would know that the message came from Jim and from no one else.

'This message is important, my master, and these are your own words that I carry to Dain Waris.'

Jim took the silver ring which Stein had given him and gave it to Tamb' Itam.

'Give this to him. He will know it comes from me.'

Jim then sent a message to Brown: 'You may go. I have many armed men protecting Patusan. You will have no chance in a fight against us, so go in peace, as you have promised me.'

Brown read the note. He laughed and tore it in small pieces.

Then Cornelius said to him,

'One thing you don't know. They have a party of armed men waiting for you down the river.'

Brown didn't believe that Jim would trick him, but Cornelius said, 'I know another way out of the river—a small stream which passes behind Dain Waris and his men. This Dain Waris is the man who fired on you when you first came to Patusan. I can lead you safely past the camp without anyone seeing us.'

33

THE DEATH OF DAIN WARIS

If anything happened to Dain Waris Doramin would kill Jim, because he was the man who decided to let Brown go free. Cornelius knew that. Although Brown had not killed Jim, as Cornelius had hoped he would, he could now lead Brown to Dain Waris.

Meanwhile Tamb' Itam had arrived at Dain Waris's camp.

'The news is good,' he said to Dain Waris. 'The white men are to be allowed to pass down the river in peace.'

Dain Waris took the ring which Lord Jim had sent and put it on his finger. 'We will return to Patusan this afternoon,' he said, 'as soon as we have seen this Brown go on his way.'

It was then that Brown showed his nature. Quietly he landed his men behind Dain Waris's camp and led them to attack.

Cornelius was suddenly frightened; he was not allowed to go home. He was pushed in front of Brown. They crept up quietly to the unsuspecting enemy. Then Brown gave the sign, and his men all fired at once into the camp. Many men were hit, and the men who were not killed by the first shots ran madly away, some into the river and some into the forest behind them.

At the sound of the shots Dain Waris jumped up and ran out on to the shore. He was shot down as Brown's men fired a second time.

Tamb' Itam fell to the ground, pretending to be dead. He saw the white men disappear as quickly and as silently as they had come.

34

THE END OF CORNELIUS

When all was quiet Tamb' Itam got to his feet. The only moving thing he could see was Cornelius. Brown had left him behind. Cornelius was running down to the river in the hope of getting one of the boats into the water.

When he saw Tamb' Itam, he threw himself on the ground, begging for mercy.

Tamb' Itam killed him. He struck at him twice with his knife and left him where he lay.

He knew that he must take this terrible news to Lord Jim at the fort. When he arrived back at Patusan, people were out looking for the return of Dain Waris and his men. Everyone was joyful because they had got rid of Captain Brown without any killing.

Tamb' Itam ran fast to the fort, and the first person he met was Jewel. He whispered to her, 'They have killed Dain Waris and many of his men.'

Jewel cried, 'Shut the gates! Oh! Doramin! He will attack us. There will be no forgiveness! Call Lord Jim!' She was trembling.

Tamb' Itam ran to his master.

'This, Lord, is a day of evil—a cursed day.' And he told his fearful story.

'We must follow them, catch them—now we must fight them,' Jim cried. But Tamb' Itam stood still.

'Why do you stand there? Waste no time!'

'Forgive me, Lord, but it is not safe for me to go out amongst the people. They will blame you. It was you who let these wicked men go free.'

Then Jim understood. Once again his world fell in ruins about him. Everything was gone this time. He, who had once been unfaithful to his honour, had now once again lost all men's trust. His first mistake was leaving his ship, and now again, a worse thing, his friend killed because of his refusal to fight, and so it was not even safe for his own servant to go out.

Jewel came in and found him with his face in his hands, utterly lost.

Tamb' Itam said to Jewel. 'There is a great deal of

weeping outside, and anger too. We shall have to fight.'

Jim looked up. 'Fight? What for?'

'For our lives, Lord.'

'I have no life.'

Tamb' Itam said, 'We must try to escape.'

But Jewel stood looking down at Jim. 'Fight!' she said.

Jim got up. 'Open the gates,' he called, and turning to his men in the courtyard he said, 'Go to your homes, all of you. There is no need for you to stay here now.'

35

'TIME TO FINISH THIS'

To Doramin's house, four men came carrying the body of Dain Waris. They laid him at Doramin's feet, and the old man sat still for a long time looking down at his dead son. Then he slowly leaned forward and took the silver ring off the cold stiff finger. A murmur of fear and sorrow was heard from the people with him, at the sight of this familiar ring. They all knew that it belonged to Jim and could only have come from Jim.

About this time Jim looked at Tamb' Itam and said, 'Time to finish this.'

'Lord?' said Tamb' Itam. He did not understand what Jim meant.

Jim walked out of the fort. Jewel ran after him. 'Will you fight?' she asked. 'Fight for our lives?'

'There is nothing to fight for.'

'Will you escape?' she cried again.

'There is no escape,' he said.

'You are going to leave me?' Jewel was watching him. He bent his head. 'You promised never to leave me.

Why? I asked you for no promise. You promised unasked
—remember?'

'Enough, my Jewel. I am not worth having.'

She ran to him weeping, and put her arms round him.

Jim caught her arms to free himself. He bent over her
and looked tenderly into her face, and then ran from
her to a boat on the river bank. Tamb' Itam followed
him, and they crossed the river.

Jim did not look back. Jewel had fallen on her knees
with her head in her hands. When they reached Doramin's
shore, Jim said,

'Do not come any further with me.'

Tamb' Itam stood still, waited a short time and then
followed behind his master.

It was beginning to grow dark. Torches twinkled here
and there. People let Jim pass, they seemed shocked
and were silent.

He came to Doramin, who was still sitting in his chair,
with a pair of pistols on his knees.

Doramin did not lift his head and Jim stood silently
in front of him for a time. Then he came up slowly to
the body and looked at his dead friend and turned back
to Doramin.

He heard whispers from the crowd. 'He has come to
take the blame.'

'Yes,' he answered them, 'I am to blame.' Then he
looked at Doramin and said gently, 'I have come to you
in sorrow, I have come ready and unarmed.'

The old man struggled to rise to his feet, and his two
young men helped him up. There were tears pouring
down his face. As he rose, the ring fell and rolled against
Jim's foot.

Poor Jim looked down at the small silver thing that
had opened the door of fame, love and success for him.

Then he stood straight with bared head and looked Doramin in the face.

Doramin, holding his pistol, lifted his right hand slowly, and taking aim shot his son's friend through the heart.

Jim looked all around at the people and they saw that he was proud and unafraid. Then with his hands over his lips he fell forward, dead.

QUESTIONS

1   1 What kind of books did Jim like best?—Stories of —
      2 What did Jim decide to be?
      3 What did Jim's father promise to do?—To try to get Jim —

2   1 Why was Jim often sent as "look-out"?—Because of—
      2 What was Jim in all his dreams?
      3 Where was Jim when the boat moved away?

3   1 How many men did the boys save?
      2 Jim told himself that he was not — What?

4   1 How long was Jim on the training ship?
      2 What rank did Jim soon reach?
      3 What happened when part of the mast fell?—It broke —

5   1 In what part of the world was Jim in hospital?
      2 How many other men were in the hospital room?
      3 Why was life easier in the East?—There were short — and more —
      4 Who owned the Patna?
      5 How many passengers were there?
      6 Who were the passengers?
      7 How many Europeans were there on the Patna?
      8 How many men steered the ship?

6   1 When did the captain come up to the bridge?
      2 Who came up after the captain?
      3 Why did the engineer shout in pain?—Because he had —

7   Are these *true* or *untrue*?
      1 Jim stayed on the bridge all the time.
      2 He was sure that there was a big hole in the ship.
      3 There were enough life-boats for all the passengers.
      Choose A or B as an answer.
      1 Jim said that there was no chance of (A. speaking to the captain;
         B. water coming into the ship; C. saving the ship.)
      2 Jim expected the pilgrims to wake up when (A. the engines stopped;
         B. his knees shook; C. the captain spoke.)
      3 (A. The two engineers; B. Jim; C. The passengers) helped the captain
         with the boat.

74

8
  1 What were the captain and the engineers doing?
  2 What ropes did Jim start cutting?—Those that held—
  3 When he was in the boat, Jim wanted to — What?

9
  1 Who said that he saw the Patna go down?
  2 The captain and engineers did not know that Jim was the fourth man in the boat. Who did they think he was?
  3 What would Jim do if the others attacked him?

10
  1 What could Jim see from the boat in the morning?
  2 What did the captain want to plan?
  3 How did the three men make a shelter from the sun?
  4 Which ship picked them up?
  5 Where was the Patna?
  6 What chance had Jim missed?

11
  1 Who called the captain a coward?
  2 What did the captain do when he left the office?
  3 What happened to the chief engineer?

12
  1 What was the enquiry about?
  2 Who did Jim speak to outside the court?
  3 What was Jim accused of?

13
  1 Who wanted to hear Jim's story?
  2 What did Jim expect to do after the enquiry?
  3 What did the court take away from Jim?

14 Are these *true* or *untrue*?
  1 Marlow found Jim on a ship.
  2 Marlow immediately asked questions.
  3 Marlow's letter asked a friend to give Jim work.

15
  1 Where did Marlow's friend give Jim work?
  2 What was the cruel blow?—It was when —
  3 Why did Jim leave a note for the old man?

16
  1 Who employed Jim at Bangkok?
  2 Why did Jim leave Bangkok?
  3 What didn't Egstrom know about Jim?

17
  1 Why did the officer want to have a quarrel?
  2 What did he tell Jim?—That everybody —
  3 How did Jim leave that place?—In —

18
  1 Why did Marlow go to see Stein?
  2 What was Stein's word for Jim?—He called Jim a —
  3 When did Stein mention Patusan?

19   1 Where was Patusan?
    2 Who was Stein's manager at Patusan before Jim went there?
    3 Who might try to kill Jim?

20   1 What two things did Stein give to Jim?
    2 Why was Jim so happy to have the ring?—It was a sign of—
    3 How long did Jim expect to stay at Patusan?

21   Choose A or B or C as an answer.
    1 Jim left the ship (A. at Patusan; B. on a sandbank; C. at the mouth of the river.)
    2 The river flowed (A. round; B. between; C. over) the two hills.
    3 The Raja's men did not kill Jim because (A. they liked him; B. they were afraid to; C. he had a pistol.)
    4 Jim (A. broke through; B. jumped over; C. ran past) the fence.
    5 He was covered with mud from (A. the Raja's house; B. the prison; C. the river.)

22   1 Who was the very large man?
    2 Who was Doramin's enemy?
    3 What was the name of the wandering Arab?
    4 What did Doramin recognise?
    5 Who used to help Doramin to stand up?
    6 Who became Jim's special friend?

23   1 When did Cornelius start cheating Stein?
    2 Why did the girl refuse to call Cornelius 'father'?
    3 How did Cornelius try to frighten Jim?—He said that the Raja—
    4 What did Jim plan to do?
    5 To destroy the fort, where would the guns have to be?
    6 If they destroyed Sherif Ali, they would also frighten another enemy. Who?

24   1 Who woke Jim?
    2 Where were the men?
    3 Why did Jim shoot the first man?

25   1 Where did Jim make the men walk?
    2 Where did they jump?
    3 What did Jim suddenly realise?

26   1 What did they use to pull the guns up?
    2 Where was Doramin?
    3 Where were the guns at sunrise?

27   1 What is the English for "Tuan"?
    2 What name did Jim give to the girl? Why?
    3 Why did Cornelius expect a "present"?

28   Are these *true* or *untrue*?
1 Jim's people were his slaves.
2 There was peace for three years.
3 Brown was the leader of a crew of criminals.

29   1 Where did Doramin send Dain Waris?
2 Which two men went to see Brown?
3 What did Cornelius want Brown to do?

30   1 What did Brown really plan to do?
2 What did the noise in Patusan mean?
3 Brown asked, 'How can I talk to him?' What was Cornelius's answer?

31   1 Why did Brown hate Jim?
2 How did Brown find a 'weak spot' in Jim?—Brown asked—
3 'Even a trapped rat can bite.' What did Brown mean?

32   1 What did Jim persuade Doramin to do?—To let—
2 Why did Jim give the ring to Tamb' Itam?—To show—
3 Who told Brown about Dain Waris?

33   1 What news did Tamb' Itam take to Dain Waris?
2 How did Tamb' Itam escape?

34   1 What was the end of Cornelius?
2 Who did Tamb' Itam meet first?
3 Why was it not safe for Tamb' Itam to go among the people?— Because they would—
4 What did Jewel want Jim to do?

35   Choose A or B or C as an answer.
1 Doramin took the ring from (A. Dain Waris's finger; B. Lord Jim; C. Tamb' Itam.)
2 'Do not come any further with me.' Tamb' Itam (A. obeyed; B. turned back; C. disobeyed.)
3 When Jim arrived, Doramin (A. looked at him; B. did not look at him; C. looked at the torches.)
4 At the end Jim was (A. a coward; B. brave; C. full of fear.)